JUMP
•INTO•
CHAPTERS™

This Book
Belongs To:

_____

_____

ANDY,

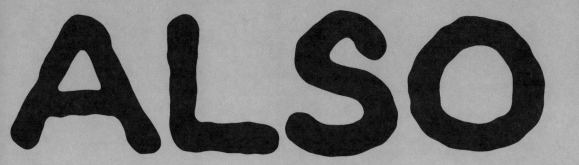

ALSO

MAXWELL EATON III

BLUE APPLE

FOR KEE

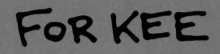
A **JUMP** • INTO • **CHAPTERS** Book™

Copyright © 2014 Maxwell Eaton III
All rights reserved/CIP data is available.
Published in the United States 2014 by
Blue Apple Books, 515 Valley Street,
Maplewood, NJ 07040
www.blueapplebooks.com
First Edition 09/14
Printed in China
ISBN: 978-1-60905-457-1 (hardcover edition)
ISBN: 978-1-60905-553-0 (paperback edition)

2 4 6 8 10 9 7 5 3 1

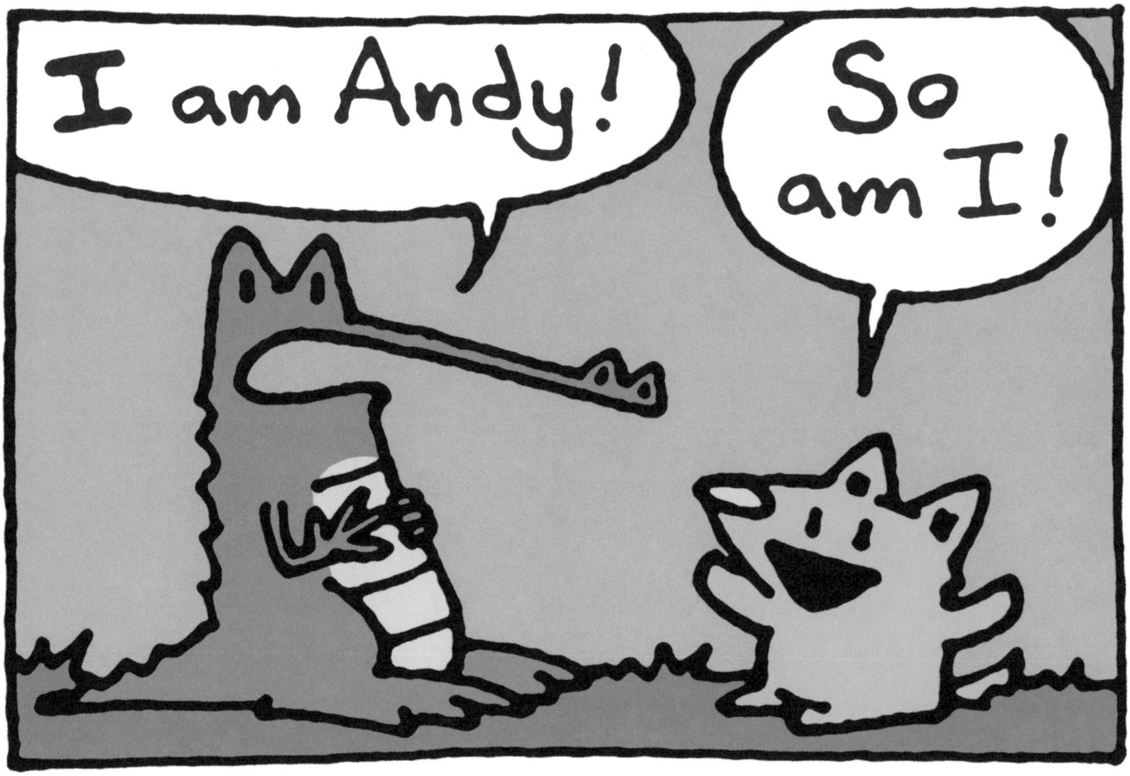
I am Andy!
So am I!

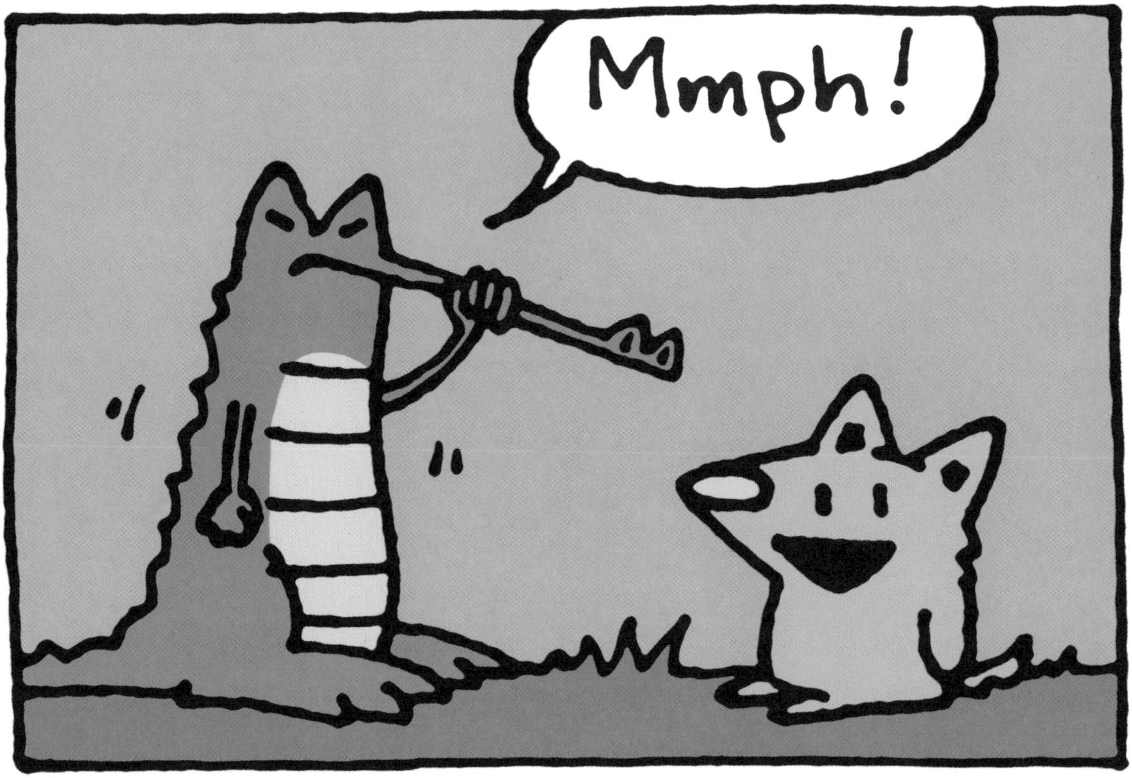
Mmph!

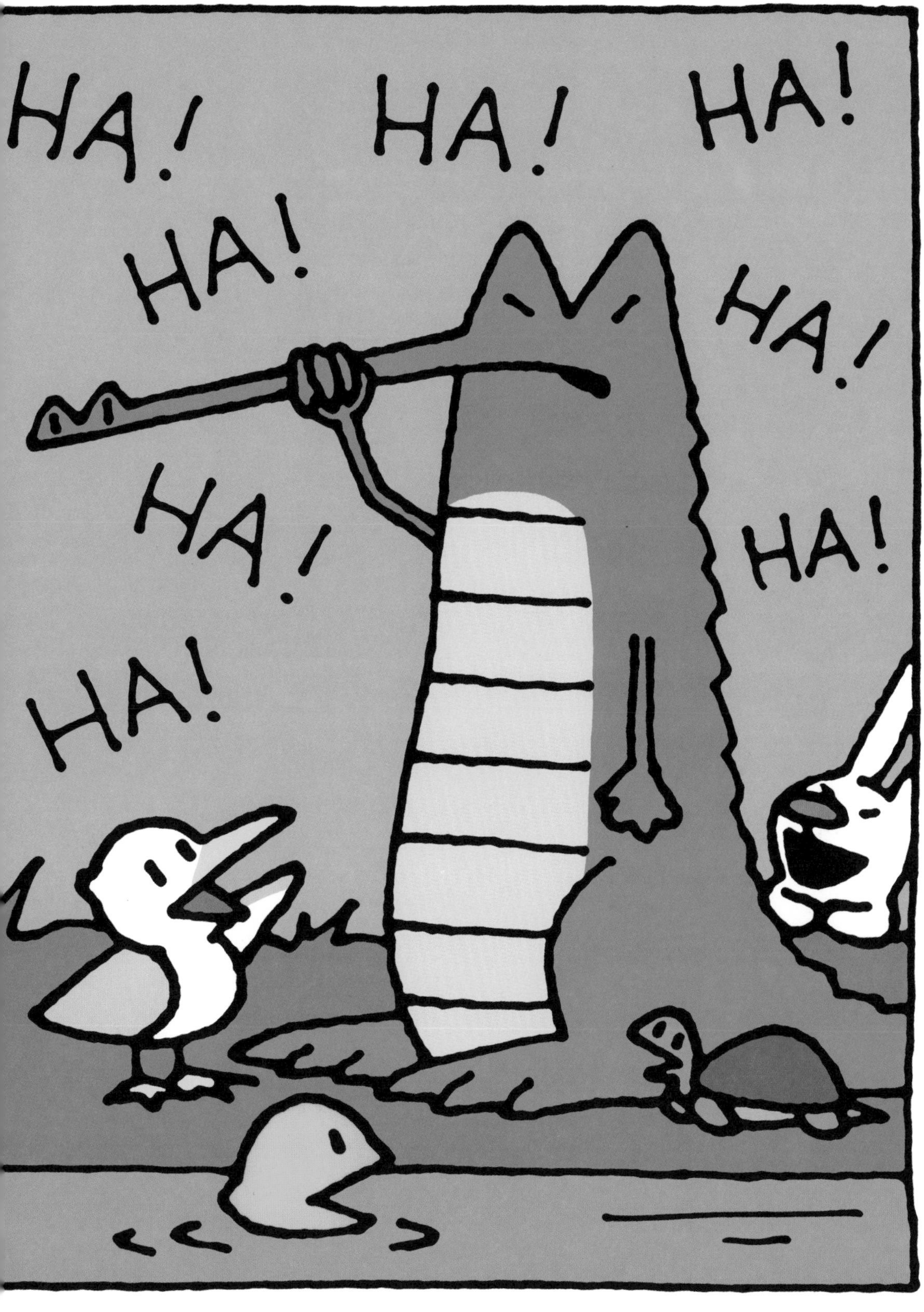
HA! HA! HA!
HA!
HA!
HA!
HA!
HA!